Danny's Castle

written and photographed
by
Mia Coulton

I have a castle.

I play castle
with my friend Abby.

We go into the castle.

I look out the window.

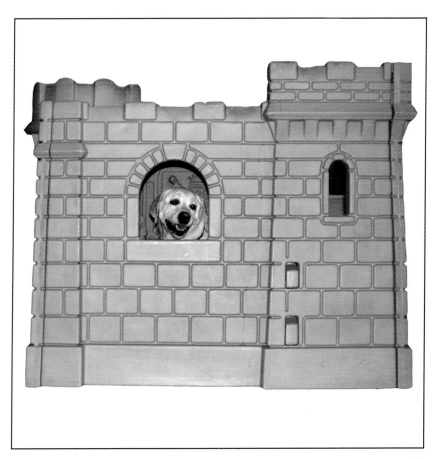

Abby looks

out the window with me.

Sometimes we dress up.

Look at me.
I am a king.

Look at Abby.

She is a princess.

Look, look!

It is Bee.

Bee is a little king.

We have fun playing castle.